To Harvey

KOSTAS THE ROOSTER

KOSTAS THE ROOSTER

by Traudl
Illustrated by
Jerry Pinkney

Lothrop, Lee & Shepard Co., Inc., New York

Text copyright © 1968 by Traudl Flaxman
Illustrations copyright © 1968 by Jerry Pinkney
Book designed by Jerry Pinkney
Library of Congress Catalog Card Number: 68-14071
Manufactured in the United States of America

1 2 3 4 5 72 71 70 69 68

Kostas the rooster lived in a little Greek village.
Every morning it was his job to wake all the villagers.

79357

It was a very difficult job.
At five o'clock he crowed to
wake the baker to bake the bread.
At six o'clock he crowed to wake
the fishermen to catch the fish.
At seven o'clock he crowed to
wake the children to go to school.
Sometimes Kostas felt that the
job was almost too difficult for him.
Sometimes he felt that it was
making him unhappy to have to
crow at just the right time...in
just the right number of crows.
Sometimes he wanted to crow a
little bit later...or a little bit earlier.
On his bad mornings he didn't
feel like crowing at all. And on
his good mornings he could have
crowed all day!

One morning Kostas did not wake up. He just slept
and slept. The baker, the fishermen, the school
children, and all the villagers just slept and slept.
Kostas dreamed that all the villagers got up on time.
He dreamed that he lived on top of the mountain and
that he did not have to worry about crowing at just
the right time. He dreamed beautiful dreams all morning.

When the sun was hot in the sky, the baker broke out
of bed and cried, "My bread isn't baked!"
The three fishermen woke. "Sweet squid," they said,
"we didn't catch any fish!"
The children woke and looked out the window. "We are
late for school," they moaned. "The teacher will beat us for sure!"

All the villagers were angry with Kostas.
"Whoever heard of a rooster not crowing on time?"
said the baker. "You crow at five o'clock tomorrow
morning, or you'll be in ROOSTER STEW!"
Kostas worried all day. He went to sleep early that
evening, to be sure to wake at five o'clock in the morning.
In the middle of the night, Kostas woke up. His eyes
opened only a crack wide. No one will sleep too late
today, he thought. "Cock-a-doodle-doo, cock-a-doodle-
doo," he crowed with his eyes half shut.

"Why am I so tired this morning?" yawned the baker as he pulled on his trousers.

The three fishermen poked each other in bed. "Wake up! Let's not miss our net of fish *this* morning."

Very sleepily, the children got dressed for school.

No one noticed that it was only the middle of the night. The fishermen were first to go outside. They looked at the black sky.

"Sweet swordfish," said the first fisherman, "do you see the moon?"

"Oh, my oyster," answered the second fisherman, "it is black as night this morning!"

"Oily octopus," cried the third fisherman, "it *is* night!"

All the villagers were very angry with Kostas. "We'll
give you one more chance," said the baker. "If you
crow wrong again, it's off with your head for sure!"
Everyone went back to sleep... everyone except
Kostas... he was too worried to sleep.
A few hours later, two masked robbers slowly crept
into the village, with bags to carry off the village
treasures. Kostas saw the robbers and crowed,
"Cock-a-doodle-doo, cock-a-doodle-doo,"
with all his strength!

The three fishermen woke with a start. "Kostas is crowing and it's still dark," they cried. The baker woke with a start. "Into the stew with Kostas!" he yelled and ran outside to catch him.

The baker caught Kostas by his neck. Kostas crowed louder and louder as the robbers stole away. But the baker became angrier and only squeezed Kostas more and more.

"We'll eat no oily octopus today," sang the first fisherman.

"We'll eat no sweet squid today," sang the second fisherman.

"We'll eat rooster stew, rooster stew!" sang the third fisherman.

The loud crowing and singing woke the children and the villagers. The children looked out of the window and saw the baker raise an ax over Kostas' head ... and out of the corners of their eyes ... they saw ... the robbers creeping away.

"Stop!" screamed the children. "Robbers ... thieves! Catch them!"

The baker was so surprised, he dropped
Kostas and ran after the robbers.
The three fishermen grabbed a fish net and ran after
the robbers. The villagers ran after the fishermen.
They came closer … and closer … the fishermen raised
their net … SWOOOOOSH … the robbers were
caught in the net. The three fishermen tied them up as
if they were two sharks.

"After running to catch robbers I get hungry!" said the first fisherman into the baker's ear.

"After running to catch robbers I feel like eating rooster stew!" said the second fisherman into the baker's ear.

"WHERE is our rooster stew?" shouted the third fisherman into the baker's ear. The three fishermen stared at the baker with angry faces.

"Kostas . . . escaped," answered the baker in a tiny voice. "But I'll catch him," he added quickly and dashed off to find Kostas.

But Kostas was hiding behind
the children.
"You'll eat no rooster stew
today," sang the children.
"You may eat a swordfish. You
may eat a squid. You may eat an
octopus. But you will not eat
Kostas...after what he did."
"What he did?" said the baker,
ax in hand. "He crowed wrong
again. *That's* what he did!"
The children spoke up loud and
clear. "No, no. Kostas crowed to
wake us, because the robbers
were here!"

"That's right," said the villagers.

"Squashy squid," said the first fisherman, "*Kostas* saved us from the robbers."

"Crunchy crab," said the second fisherman, "Kostas is a HERO!"

"Clumped clam," said the third fisherman, "we almost *ate* a hero!"

The three fishermen lifted Kostas high into the air and everyone, even the baker, cheered, "BRAVO, KOSTAS, BRAVO!"

The villagers were very happy
with Kostas. They were so happy
that they cheered for Kostas all
the way to his new home on top of
the mountain.
There, he could crow a little bit
later ... or a little bit earlier.
On his bad mornings he didn't
have to crow at all. On his
good mornings he could crow all
day. And if he saw any robbers,
he could dash down the mountain
and warn the villagers.

For a special rooster like Kostas,
that was an easy job.